NONNA'S PORCH

RITA GRAY
ILLUSTRATED BY TERRY WIDENER

HYPERION BOOKS FOR CHILDREN

NEW YORK

Printed in Singapore

First Edition

1 3 5 7 9 10 8 6 4 2

Reinforced binding

This book is set in BGothic.

The art for this book was created using Golden Acrylics on Strathmore Bristol Board.

Library of Congress Cataloging-in-Publication Data on file.

ISBN 0-7868-1613-9

Visit www.hyperionbooksforchildren.com

To our nonna
— R.G.

In honor of "Camp Finney"
— T.W.

Nonna's porch is very still,
Except for the sound of her rocking chair . . .

CREAK
CREAK
CREAK
CREAK

Rocking to and fro.

Nonna's porch is very still,
     Except for the sound of her knitting needles . . .

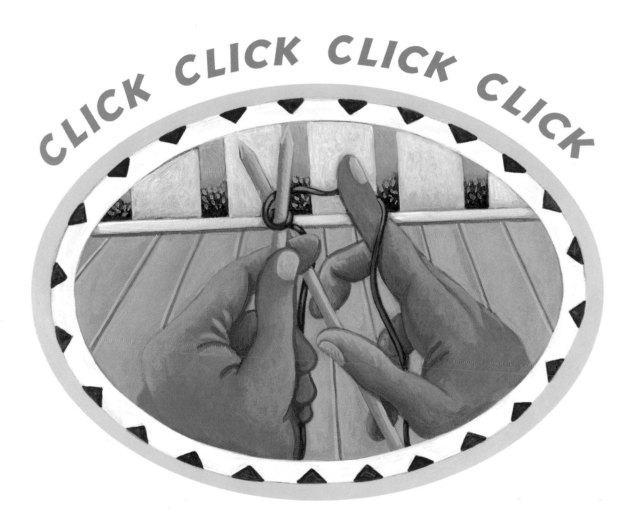

CLICK CLICK CLICK CLICK

Knitting in a row.

Nonna's porch is very still,
   Except for the sound of a red bird . . .

WHAT-CHEER

CHEER CHEER

Singing in its nest.

Nonna's porch is very still,
Except for the sound of a spotted fawn . . .

PLUCK

PLUCK

PLUCK

PLUCK

Petals taste the best.

Nonna's porch is very still,
   Except for the sound of a brave chipmunk . . .

CHIP

CHIP

CHIP

CHIP

All he does is chatter.

Nonna's porch is very still,
  Except for the sound of running feet . . .

PITTA-PAT   PITTA-PAT

And all the animals scatter!

Nonna's porch is very still,
   Except for the sound of shucking corn . . .

squeeaaaak! POP!

squeeaaaak! POP!

Golden ears lie bare.

Nonna's porch is very still,
   Except for the sound of our backyard game . . .

"Ready or not, here I come!"

Hiding everywhere.

Nonna's porch is very still,
    Except for the sound of lemon and ice . . .

TINK-A-TINK

TINK-A-TINK

Swirling in a glass.

Nonna's porch is very still,
Except for the sound of
rainbow spray . . .

Whooooooosssssssssiyyysshhh

Arched across the grass.

Nonna's porch is very still,
Except for the sound of garden peas . . .

SNAP!

PLINK! PLINK!
PLINK!

Dropping from a shell.

Nonna's porch is very still,
Except for the sound
of our family feast . . .

Mmmmmmmmmmmmmmm

And so many stories
to tell.

Nonna's porch is very still,
    Except for the sound of a cricket's call . . .

CHIRP

CHIRP

CHIRP

CHIRP

He's hidden, out of sight.

Nonna's porch is very still,
  Except for the sound of masked raccoons . . .

rustle shuff shuff shuff

Bandits in the night.

Nonna's porch is very still,
   Except for the sound of Nonna's heart . . .

TA-TUM, TA-TUM

TA-TUM, TA-TUM

It keeps a steady beat.

Nonna's porch is very still,
   Except for the sound of her rocking chair . . .

CREAK

CREAK

CREAK

CREAK

Rocking me to sleep.